MINTON

goes TRUCKING

ANNA FIENBERG
and
KIM GAMBLE

ALLEN & UNWIN

'*B*eep *beep beep*,' Minton burbled in his sleep.

'If you want a job,' the man at the building site had said, 'you'll need a dump truck.'

Minton longed to shovel and dig. He yearned to scoop and carry. He had already made the truck, but how would the dumper lift up?

'*Heave slide dump*,' he panted through his dreams.

'Sssh!' hissed Turtle in the dark, giving him a prod. But Minton went on beeping and dumping.

In the morning Minton sprang up and clapped Turtle on the shell. 'I've got it!' he cried. 'I know exactly how to do it! I saw it all in a dream.'

'The best thing to do with a dream,' said Turtle, 'is to forget it. Listen to me, I know.'

But Minton was already out the door.

*H*e headed for the caravan where the beetle trainer lived.

'Have you had breakfast yet?' the trainer asked suspiciously.

'Oh yes, yes, thank you!' said Minton. He tried not to look too closely at the beetles. They made his mouth water. Beetle *sauce*.

'The thing is, you see,' Minton went on quickly, 'I want to borrow something from your act.'

'Oh?' said the trainer. He was busy teaching a beetle called Rolf to do a full spin on the trapeze. Rolf looked nervous. The trainer gave him a push.

'Catch her by the front legs!' he urged Rolf, as the beetle swung through the air to meet his partner, Babette.

Minton eyed the swing with enthusiasm.

'That's a magnificent trapeze,' he said. 'What's it made of—paperclips?'

'That's right,' said the trainer, trying to untangle the beetles' legs. 'Flippin' feelers!'

'Well, could I have one? A paperclip, that is. I only need one.'

While the beetle trainer went to find a spare, Minton looked at Rolf. Rolf looked at Minton.

'Beetle sauce,' thought Minton.

Minton carried the paperclip carefully back to the caravan. Turtle opened an eye.

'Bingo!' said Minton, holding up his treasure. 'Here's my dumping lever!'

Turtle closed an eye. 'That thing'll never work and you'll get caught beneath it and the dumper will come crashing down and you'll be flattened like a mosquito. But don't listen to me, will you. You never do.'

Minton rummaged through his toolbox and found a fine wooden skewer. He hummed softly as he opened the paperclip and stuck it to the skewer. Then he flipped one end of the clip up and down. It tipped the dumper perfectly. He flipped it again. Easy as snapping your fingers.

'I could do this all afternoon!' crowed Minton.

'You'd better not,' said Turtle, 'or we'll never get the job.'

'Does that mean you're coming with me?'

'I suppose so,' said Turtle, yawning. '*Some*one has to earn a living around here.'

At the building site, a new house was going up. An excavator was demolishing the concrete gutter, to make a driveway. Minton and Turtle climbed down from their truck and the foreman called them over.

'See this sand heap?' said the foreman.
'I want you to build castles, big ones, with turrets
and a moat and bridges and tunnels. There's a lot
of sand to move—think you can do it?'

'Are you joking?' asked Turtle. 'That's
easy-peasy for an expert like Minton.'

Just then the long mechanical arm of the excavator swung round and reached out towards Turtle.

'*Aaargh!*' Turtle was scooped up with a load of broken concrete. His shell scraped against the sharp teeth of the bucket. Turtle was lurching higher and higher into the sky. Any minute he was going to be dropped—like a pebble from a cliff.

Suddenly the excavator swivelled round
and he was flung to the other side of the bucket.
He peered through the spiky teeth. The ground
looked very far away. He could hardly see
Minton's yellow spots. Then he felt the bucket
grinding beneath him. It was starting to split
open, ready to empty its load!

'Turtle soup!' he wailed.

Minton scrambled up into the cabin of the excavator. 'Stop!' he cried to the driver. 'Stop! Your machine has swallowed my friend!'

The driver lowered the bucket and turned off the engine. He peered in and poked Turtle's shell with his finger.

'Sorry, mate,' he said, rubbing his chin. 'Thought you were just a rock.'

Turtle sniffed and crawled out. 'Just a rock! He's got rocks in his *head* if you ask me,' he told Minton.

Minton worked all afternoon. Turtle helped him load up the truck and Minton dumped great piles of sand to make the skyscraper castles.

They dug lakes and rivers and made islands
of smooth pebbles, joined by bridges. Lights were
beginning to shine in the houses around them,
just as they were finishing.

'Good work,' said the foreman. 'That's just what I need to make people stop and look at my sign.'

Bob Button Builds Best

'Minton and Turtle Do All the Hard Work, it should say,' muttered Turtle.

As Minton and Turtle drove back to their caravan, Turtle sighed.

'Are you tired?' asked Minton.

'Yes, even my shell is aching,' said Turtle. 'But don't mind about me, I'm used to being exhausted. No, the worst thing was working with that sand today. It made me homesick. Didn't it make you think of our beach? Don't you miss it?'

Now Minton sighed. 'Yes,' he said quietly. 'I do.'

'Me too. I miss the feel of the sea, all slippery and cool, and napping under the palm trees. What do you miss most?'

'I miss the mornings,' said Minton. 'Raking through the sand. Seeing what has washed up. Lying in my hammock, looking at the stars.'

They both sighed.

'But we can never get back,' Turtle said gloomily. 'We're so far away.'

Minton drove home through the city traffic. He tooted his horn and stopped at the red lights and waved politely at the policeman. But he was frowning. This was the biggest problem he'd ever had.

As they walked back towards the circus, an idea swam like a bright fish right into his mind.

'Turtle,' he cried. 'I've got it!'

'Uh oh,' said Turtle, but he almost smiled.

'This time we won't go over the water. We'll go *under*! I'm going to build a submarine to take us home.'

'It'll never work,' said Turtle.
But Minton was already wondering what he
would use for a periscope.

To make Minton's truck you'll need: 2 margarine or butter tubs, a box about the same width, 4 lids, a cork, 2 skewers, 2 icy-pole sticks, a large paperclip, tape, glue, scissors or a sharp knife, and paint.

1. Make holes in tub and insert skewers

2. Unfold paperclip and tape to skewer as shown

3. Cut, fold and tape cabin, and insert front axle

4. Tape icy-pole sticks to cabin and tray

4. Drill holes in lids, paint pieces, and glue cork hubcaps and wheels. Add bumper and assemble

Happy trucking!